P9-DZY-134

FOR JOHN, ALEX, JULIANNA, AND MAX— ALWAYS!

T. S.

TO AVA (ALL THE WAY TO THE MOON) ... AND TO KATY.

A. G.

tiger tales

5 River Road, Suite 128, Wilton, CT 06897
Published in the United States 2014
Originally published in Great Britain 2014
by Little Tiger Press
Text copyright © 2014 Tammi Salzano
Illustrations copyright © 2014 Ada Grey
ISBN-13: 978-1-58925-161-8
ISBN-10: 1-58925-161-X
Printed in China
LTP/1400/0885/0314

For more insight and activities,
visit us at www.tigertalesbooks.com

I Love You Just the Way You Are

by TAMMI SALZANO

Illustrated by ADA GREY

tiger tales

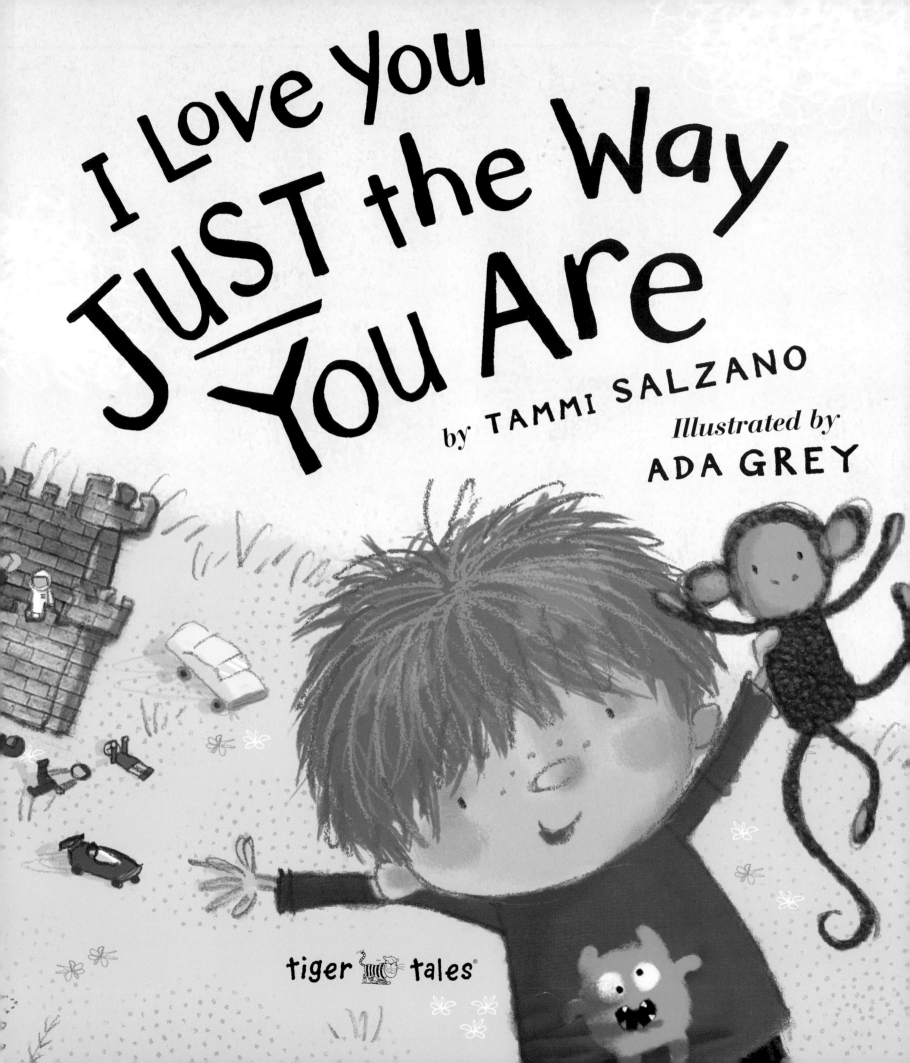

I love you in the morning when the sun shines on the day,

With silly hair that's sticking up each and every way.

I **love** you when you're playing—

b l o w i n g
bubbles

in
the
sun,

Climbing **high**

and **sliding** down, having **so** much **fun!**

I love you when you're messy —
sticky fingers, face, and hair,
With papers scattered
all around and paint
splashed
everywhere!

I love you when

we're quiet, sharing books and puzzles, too.

I treasure *every* moment of this **special** time with **you.**

I love you when you dress up

and pretend to be a king,

Or a superhero-pirate-dog

who **loves** to
dance and **sing.**

I love you when it's bath time,

squeaky-clean and smelling sweet,
Giggling as I scrub your ears,
tummy, hands, and feet.

I **love** you when it's **bedtime** and **you** **bounce** into your bed.

I hold you close
to say good night

and
kiss
you on the
head.

I love your smile, freckles, **all** the **funny** things you **say**.

I love you just the way YOU are, and more and more and more each day!